Zadie the Sewing Fairy

Special thanks to
Narinder Dhami

No part of this publication may be reproduced, stored in a retrieval system, or transmitted in any form or by any means, electronic, mechanical, photocopying, recording, or otherwise, without written permission of the publisher. For information regarding permission, write to Rainbow Magic Limited, c/o HIT Entertainment, 830 South Greenville Avenue, Allen, TX 75002-3320.

ISBN 978-0-545-70831-9

12 11 10 9 8 7 6 5 4 3 2 1   15 16 17 18 19 20/0

Printed in the U.S.A.   40

This edition first printing, March 2015

Zadie
the Sewing
Fairy

by Daisy Meadows

SCHOLASTIC INC.

The Fairyland
Palace

Sara Sketchley's
house

Bridge

Rainspell

Island

Maze

Park

Carrie's
Jewelry
Shop

Beach and
Boardwalk

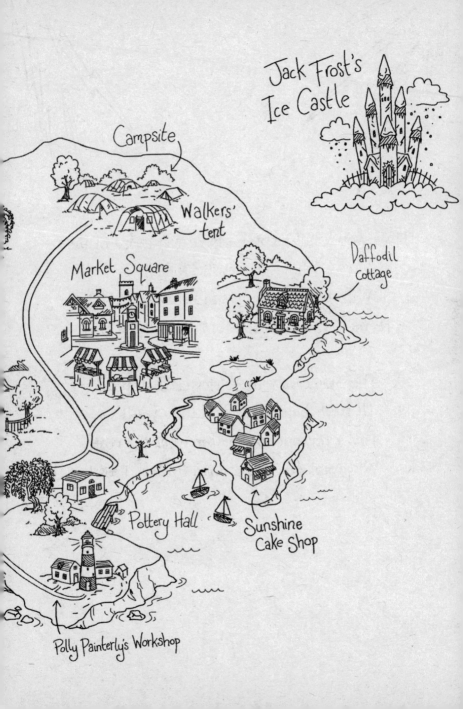

Jack Frost's
Ice Castle

Campsite

Walkers'
tent

Daffodil
Cottage

Market Square

Pottery Hall

Sunshine
Cake Shop

Polly Painterly's Workshop

I'm a wonderful painter—have you heard of me?
Behold my artistic ability!
With palette, brush, and paints in hand,
I'll be the most famous artist in all the land!

The Magical Crafts Fairies can't stop me!
I'll steal their magic, and then you'll see
That everyone, no matter what the cost,
Will want a painting done by Jack Frost!

Contents

All Thumbs

"It looks like another magical morning, Kirsty," Rachel Walker said, gazing out the window of Daffodil Cottage. Even though it was still early, the sun was already shining. Rainspell Island looked green and beautiful with the morning light glimmering on the sea.

"Are you talking about the weather or our adventures with the Magical Crafts Fairies?" Kirsty Tate asked, her eyes twinkling. They'd arrived on Rainspell Island two days earlier and the girls were spending every other night in Kirsty's little attic bedroom at the b and b with the Tates, and alternate nights with Rachel's parents at a nearby campsite. The girls loved going to Rainspell Island for vacation because it was where they'd first met and become friends with the fairies.

"Both!" Rachel replied. Then she sighed. "Wasn't it mean of Jack Frost to steal the Magical Craft Fairies' objects?"

Kirsty nodded. "It was terrible," she agreed, "especially with Crafts Week here on Rainspell *and* Magical Crafts

Week happening at the same time in Fairyland. No one will have fun doing arts and crafts if Jack Frost has his way!"

While eagerly checking out the Crafts Week activities a few days before, Rachel and Kirsty had been thrilled to meet Kayla the Pottery Fairy, one of the seven Magical Crafts Fairies. Kayla had invited them to Fairyland to see King Oberon and Queen Titania announce the opening of Magical Crafts Week. The best and most beautiful crafts produced by the fairies would decorate the Fairyland Palace! Everyone, including the girls, had been very excited.

But the opening ceremony had turned into a disaster when Jack Frost and his goblins showed up, tossing balloons filled

with bright green paint at the crowd.
Queen Titania, Kayla, and the other
Magical Crafts Fairies had been
splattered with paint! In all the
confusion, Jack Frost and the goblins had
stolen the Magical Crafts Fairies' special
objects.

Jack Frost had declared that he was the
best at every kind of craft, and that no
one else was allowed to be better than
him. Then, with a wave of his ice wand,
he and his goblins had disappeared to
the human world—taking the magic
objects with them. Rachel and Kirsty
knew that the Crafts Week on Rainspell
Island and in Fairyland would be a
complete disaster while the fairies' magic
items were missing. They'd immediately
offered to help the Magical Crafts Fairies

find the goblins and get their magic back!

"The pottery and drawing classes were so much fun," Kirsty remarked as she buttoned her favorite pink shirt. "But only because we found Kayla's magic vase and Annabelle's magic pencil sharpener just in time."

"And we'll do our best to find the other magic objects, too," Rachel said firmly. "We can't let Jack Frost ruin the whole week!"

At that moment, Mrs. Tate opened the door. "Girls, are you ready for breakfast?" she asked. Right away, Rachel noticed the pretty, full-skirted floral dress that Mrs. Tate was wearing.

"Wow, what a beautiful dress!" Rachel gasped.

Mrs. Tate looked pleased. "Thank you, Rachel," she said.

"My mom made that dress herself!" Kirsty explained proudly. "She even added those tiny little buttons down the front, and sewed in all those pleats."

Mrs. Tate laughed. "I've been taking sewing classes," she told Rachel.

"Oh, Mom," Kirsty said with a frown, "I think I need your sewing skills right now!" She'd just noticed that one of the pearly buttons on her shirt had come loose and was hanging by a thread.

"I have my sewing kit with me—I can fix that easily," said Mrs. Tate.

The girls followed her into the bedroom next door where she opened her sewing kit. She took out a spool of pink thread, a needle, and a small, silver object.

"I know that's called a thimble," Rachel said, "But I don't know what it's for!"

"It protects my finger when I push the needle through the cloth," Mrs. Tate explained. "I'll thread the needle first, and then I'll show you."

Kirsty's mom held up the needle and attempted to insert the end of the thread through the eye. It wouldn't go through! She tried again and again, even moving over to the window for extra light. But it was no use—she couldn't do it.

"Let me try," Kirsty offered. She took the needle and thread and tried to push the thread through the eye. But somehow, the thread kept missing, even though Kirsty held the needle very still. Rachel also tried, but this time the thread got tangled into a big ball.

"Oh, don't worry, Mom," Kirsty said. "I'll just change my shirt, and you can fix this one later."

"Well, making my dress was easy compared to sewing on that button!" Mrs. Tate said, shaking her head. "I seem to be all thumbs today."

Kirsty glanced at Rachel. They both knew *exactly* why Mrs. Tate was having so much trouble.

"It's because the goblins have Zadie the Sewing Fairy's magic thimble!" Rachel whispered as they headed back to Kirsty's bedroom.

"We have to find it fast," Kirsty said

anxiously. "I wonder if we'll see one of the Magical Crafts Fairies today?"

She opened the closet doors and gave a little yelp of surprise as Zadie the Sewing Fairy fluttered out!

Not Sew Easy!

Zadie hovered in front of Rachel and Kirsty with a big smile on her face. She was dressed in stylish shorts and purple leggings, with a sparkly pink vest over a white T-shirt.

"I bet you've been expecting me, girls," Zadie said. "You already know I need your help to find my magic thimble. Otherwise, no one will be able to sew *anything* anywhere!" She sighed. "I hate to even think about it!"

"Where should we start looking?" asked Kirsty.

Rachel grabbed the Crafts Week pamphlet from her nightstand and flipped through it. "It says here that Artemis Johnson is offering a sewing workshop in the market square," Rachel pointed out. "Maybe we should start there?"

"Artie Johnson is the Crafts Week organizer," Kirsty explained to Zadie.

"I think that would be a great place to start!" Zadie said eagerly. "Let's head out after breakfast."

"Oops, I almost forgot!" Kirsty said with a grin as Zadie tucked herself into

Rachel's pocket, folding her wings away.
"I have to change my shirt."

As soon as Kirsty had swapped her
pink shirt for a white one, the girls ran
downstairs. They quickly ate some
cereal, and then asked to be excused.

"I bet you're excited to get to your next
activity," Mr. Tate said, looking at them
over his newspaper. "What is it today?"

"Sewing," Kirsty and Rachel said
together.

"Oh, I'm *sew* happy for you!" Kirsty's
dad grinned. "Get it?"

The girls laughed and waved good-
bye. Then they left Daffodil Cottage and
headed straight toward the town.

"I can almost feel an invisible thread
pulling me toward my magic thimble!"
Zadie whispered as they approached the

square. "I'm more sure than ever that
we'll find it here somewhere."

The market square was full of booths
selling fabric, thread, and other sewing
accessories like buttons, zippers, and
ribbons. Kirsty and Rachel were
fascinated by the heaps of shimmering
fabric in every color under the sun, and
the big spools of shiny, colored ribbon.
One booth had trays of antique buttons

made of wood, porcelain, and green
jade. The girls kept a sharp eye out for
Zadie's thimble, but they didn't see
it—and they didn't see any goblins,
either!

In the middle of the square was a
long, wooden table where the sewing
workshop was being held. There was a
large group of kids seated at the table
piled with fabric and thread. Artie was

moving around from one to another, checking on the progress of their projects. As Rachel and Kirsty headed over, Artie spotted them and waved.

"Good to see you girls again!" she said happily. "Come and join us." She pointed to two empty chairs. "Sewing is my favorite craft, you know," Artie went on. "I'm hoping a sewing project will win a prize at the end of Crafts Week." She handed the girls some patterns. "Take a look through these projects and let me know which one you'd like to try."

Rachel chose a pattern for a shoulder bag with a big velvet flower attached to

the front, and Kirsty decided to make a
teddy bear. Then Artie helped them pick
out their materials—green and purple
velvet for Rachel, and some gold fur
fabric for Kirsty's teddy.

"No sign of goblins yet," Zadie
murmured from inside Rachel's pocket as
the girls cut out their pattern pieces.
"Keep looking, girls!"

Rachel and Kirsty began to sew, but
soon it became clear that things were
going wrong all around them! There
were cries from the other kids as fabric
ripped, threads snapped, zippers got
stuck, and buttons fell off. Artie ran
around, trying to help everyone, but she
was looking very stressed-out.

Kirsty began stuffing her teddy
bear—but to her horror, the seams she'd
just sewn so carefully came
apart. All the
stuffing fell
right out!

Rachel
finished
attaching
the strap of
her shoulder bag, but

as soon as she put the bag down on the table, the strap fell off again.

Artie groaned. "This sewing workshop is a total disaster!"

Rachel and Kirsty exchanged worried glances. They knew exactly why everything was going wrong!

No Green to Be Seen!

Rachel could feel Zadie shifting around uneasily in her pocket and guessed that the little fairy was upset about what was happening. Then a boy sitting across from them suddenly gave a squeal of surprise.

"Where did my green fabric go?" the boy cried, hunting around on the table. "It was just here a minute ago!"

"It probably got buried under the other material," Artie told him.

Rachel reached for some green velvet to make a new strap for her shoulder bag. To her amazement, it was snatched from right under her nose!

"Where did that green velvet go?" Rachel exclaimed, bewildered.

Kirsty was choosing some buttons to use as decoration for her teddy bear. But when she leaned over to pick up two green buttons, she found herself grabbing at empty air.

"All the green things seem to keep disappearing!" Rachel murmured. "There's no green fabric, thread, buttons, ribbons, or zippers left."

"It *must* have something to do with the goblins," said Kirsty. "After all, green is their favorite color! But why didn't we see them?"

The girls looked around for goblins. They couldn't see any, but Rachel did spot a trail of green fabric, ribbons, zippers, and buttons leading across the market square.

"They went that way!" she whispered to Kirsty, pointing out the trail.

Both girls jumped up from their chairs.

"We're just going to look around the booths for a few things we need for our projects," Rachel told Artie. "We'll be back soon."

"That's fine," said Artie.

The girls rushed off. As soon as they were out of sight behind a booth, Zadie zoomed out of Rachel's pocket.

"Nice job spotting that trail of green, girls!" she cried. "Let's fly around and look for goblins."

Zadie waved her wand and surrounded Rachel and Kirsty with sparkling fairy magic. The girls felt themselves becoming smaller and smaller until they were the same size as Zadie, with their own shiny fairy wings.

Zadie quickly fluttered out from

behind the booth with Rachel and Kirsty close behind. Together, the three friends flew through the market, keeping out of sight while they searched for goblins. They darted over, under, and between colorful fabrics that hung above the booths, billowing in the breeze. The whole time, they were looking for any signs of goblin activity.

Suddenly, Kirsty spotted a huge bundle of green fabric. It seemed to be moving quickly through the market square all by itself.

"How strange!" Kirsty exclaimed, pointing it out to Rachel and Zadie. "We should take a closer look."

Zadie and the girls swooped down near the bundle of fabric. As they did, Rachel noticed a pair of enormous, shiny green shoes almost hidden beneath the pieces of fabric.

"There's a goblin under there!" Rachel whispered.

"That must be how he managed to steal all the green things from our sewing workshop," Kirsty murmured. "He hid under piles of fabric!"

"He's heading to that quiet corner over there," Zadie said, pointing with her wand.

The goblin was hurrying to the outskirts of the market, toward a booth half hidden behind a few flower arrangements in big pots. Rachel, Kirsty, and Zadie followed him, being careful to stay out of sight. The booth was already piled high with green fabric, buttons, zippers, ribbons, and thread, but the goblin began adding the things he'd been carrying to the teetering pile.

"Look, there are

more of them!" Kirsty whispered as she noticed three other goblins close by.

The goblins were having fun with fabric. One was making a tent out of shiny green satin, while the other two were playing tug-of-war with a long strip of emerald green silk.

Very quietly, Zadie, Rachel, and Kirsty flew over to perch on the awning above the booth.

"I wonder which one of these goblins has my thimble," Zadie said. "We're very close now, girls. I can feel my thimble's magic!"

Just then, Kirsty noticed someone else strutting around below them.

"Who's that?" Kirsty murmured, raising her eyebrows as she stared at his garish green pin-striped suit and enormous green felt hat. But the brim of the hat was pulled down very low, so Kirsty couldn't see the face underneath it.

"Look at his shoes!" Zadie whispered. The girls noticed the same large, shiny green shoes that the goblins were wearing. "He's a goblin, too!"

"I sewed this outfit all by

myself!" the goblin in the suit bragged to the others. "I made everything, even this little green handkerchief in my jacket pocket. I'm so talented! I can sew *anything*."

Rachel, Kirsty, and Zadie exchanged knowing glances.

"That goblin has my magic thimble—
that's why he can sew so well!" Zadie
declared. "But how do we get it back?"

Rachel and Kirstty were silent,
thinking hard. They needed a plan—
and fast!

Goblin Tailor

"That goblin's awfully proud of his sewing skills," Kirsty said thoughtfully. "Maybe we can use that to get the thimble from him?" She whispered a plan to Rachel and Zadie.

"Good thinking, Kirsty!" Zadie said with a bright smile. "Let's give it a try."

The three of them flew swiftly down behind the booth and out of sight. There,

Zadie returned the girls to their normal size, then hid in Rachel's pocket. Kirsty and Rachel strolled casually out from behind the booth and headed toward the goblin in the suit.

"Oh!" Rachel exclaimed loudly. All of the goblins turned to stare suspiciously at the girls. "What a *wonderful* suit! I love it!"

A big, smug grin spread across the goblin's green face. "Isn't it?" he said proudly. "I made it myself, you know. Every single stitch!"

"That's amazing," Kirsty joined in. "You must be an *incredible* tailor!"

"I am!" the goblin bragged. "I'm a sewing genius!"

"Oh, could you please teach me and my friend to sew just like you?" Rachel pleaded breathlessly. *"Please?"*

The goblin looked flattered. "Well, you'll never be as good as me," he said, "but I guess I could give you some lessons."

The goblin grabbed some

needles, thread, and fabric from the booth, then sat down on the rim of one of the big planters. The girls followed his lead. Meanwhile, the other goblins went back to their games.

"Here, thread your needles," the goblin told the girls, handing them each a spool of thread and a needle. As Kirsty took the needle from him, she gave a little yelp, pretending that she'd pricked herself with the sharp point.

"*Ow*, that hurt!" Kirsty gasped. "I'm so clumsy!" She glanced innocently at the goblin. "Do you have a thimble I can borrow to protect my finger?"

"No, I don't," the goblin snapped. "Now hurry up

and thread your needles—I don't have all day, you know!"

Kirsty glanced at Rachel in dismay as the goblin began stroking his jacket. "Look at this intricate embroidery on the lapels!" The goblin sighed with delight. "And see how perfectly straight all the hems are? This is the most beautiful suit in the whole world!" But then he frowned. "It just needs one little finishing touch . . ."

"What's that?" asked Kirsty. Even though her idea hadn't worked, she was still hoping there was some way they could get Zadie's thimble back.

"A fabulous cape, just like Jack Frost's!" the goblin declared. He ran back to the booth and began digging through the piles of fabric. "None of this is good enough," he muttered in disgust.

"What kind of fabric are you looking for?" Rachel asked.

"I want my cape to be bright green, just like me," the goblin replied. "And it should be very sparkly on the outside, but oh-so-soft on the inside."

A plan instantly popped into Rachel's head. "I've seen some special fabric exactly like that!" she announced. "We'll get it for you."

"Hooray!" the goblin cheered. He began tap-dancing happily around in his big, shiny green shoes.

The girls darted off behind the booth again, and Zadie zoomed up out of Rachel's pocket.

"Zadie, you heard what the goblin said," Rachel whispered. She grinned and raised an eyebrow. "Can you use your magic to make the soft, sparkly fabric he described? I have an idea!"

Thimble Fumble

"Sparkly on the outside, soft on the inside," Zadie repeated with a smile. "Yes, I can do that!"

She waved her wand in the air, and the girls saw a misty cloud of magic fairy dust floating around them. A long piece of beautiful green fabric appeared out of thin air and floated down into Rachel's and Kirsty's arms. The fabric was the exact same shade as the goblin's skin, and full of thin gold threads that sparkled in the sunlight.

"It's beautiful!" Kirsty exclaimed.

"And it's so soft," Rachel added, stroking the delicate fabric. "He'll love it!"

Kirsty folded up the fabric, while Zadie dove back into Rachel's pocket. Then they all hurried back to the goblin.

"Here we are!" Kirsty said, holding up the fabric with a flourish.

"Oh, wow!" the goblin gasped, wide-eyed. He reached out and gently touched the fabric. "It's so soft. It's exactly what I wanted."

He tried to take the fabric, but Kirsty

pulled it back out of his reach.

"You can only have it if you return Zadie's magic thimble," she said firmly.

The goblin's face darkened. "No! I'm not giving it to you!" he shouted, and tried to grab the fabric again. But the girls were ready for him! Kirsty dodged quickly out of his way. She began

circling the goblin and winding the
sparkling green fabric around him.
Rachel took the other end of the fabric.
Between them, the girls wrapped up the
goblin from his shoulders to his feet like
an Egyptian mummy!

"We know you have Zadie's thimble," Kirsty told the trapped goblin. "Now, where is it?"

"I won't tell you!" the goblin snapped, squirming desperately to free himself. But as he wriggled around, trying to escape, his hat fell off. Rachel spotted something shimmering on top of his head.

"It's Zadie's thimble!" Rachel gasped.

Zadie immediately flew out of Rachel's pocket and zoomed toward the thimble perched on the goblin's big green head. But before she could reach it, the goblin began yelling.

"A pesky fairy is trying to steal my magic thimble!" he shouted to the other goblins, who'd been too busy playing to notice what was going on.

The goblins all came racing over. Rachel, Kirsty, and Zadie desperately tried to grab the thimble first, but the captured goblin hopped around, trying to avoid them as best he could. Then one of the other goblins made a giant leap forward and grabbed the thimble from the top of the goblin's head.

All of the goblins whooped with triumph.

"We have to keep this safe for Jack Frost!" the goblin with the thimble

declared. He glared at Rachel, Kirsty, and Zadie. "*You* can't have it!"

"That thimble is *mine*!" said the goblin in the suit, wriggling out of the green fabric. He tried to snatch the thimble back, but the other goblin wouldn't give it up. "I need it, or I won't be able to sew my beautiful clothes anymore."

"You've had your turn," snapped the goblin with the thimble. "Now *I* want a chance to use it!"

"Me too! Me too!" the other goblins cried. They began arguing loudly.

Their squabbling gave Kirsty an idea, so she murmured a few words to Zadie and Rachel. Zadie nodded and pointed her wand at a scrap of green velvet lying on the nearby booth. A few magic sparkles instantly transformed the velvet into a gorgeous embroidered vest with a green satin lining.

The goblin with the thimble saw the

vest and his face lit up. "Oh, I wish I could make beautiful clothes like that!" He sighed, grabbing the vest and slipping it on. "And now I can, since the magic thimble is mine!"

The other goblins began yelling at him again.

"It's not yours, it's Jack Frost's!"

"I want a turn! I want to make myself a fancy green vest, too!"

"Give me that thimble back right now—I had it first!"

"Wait!" Rachel stepped in front of them. "*None* of you will be able to sew beautiful clothes if you keep arguing over the thimble like this!" She looked at

the goblins, who were all glaring back at her. "Listen, Zadie will show you *all* how to make beautiful clothes. She'll teach you how to sew—but only if you give her the magic thimble."

Rachel held her breath. Would the plan work?

Sewing Superstars!

The goblin with the thimble frowned.
He glanced at the other goblins, who all
looked interested in what Rachel was
saying.

"If we just give the thimble to Jack
Frost, we'll *never* learn how to sew!" the
goblin in the suit pointed out.

The goblin holding the thimble stroked his vest thoughtfully. Then he nodded. "All right," he agreed, reluctantly, and he offered the thimble to Zadie. With a cry of relief, the little fairy swooped down to him. The instant Zadie touched the thimble, it became fairy-sized. She popped it right onto her finger with a big smile on her face.

"Thank you," Zadie told the goblins. "But we won't start our sewing lessons now, because you shouldn't have stolen my thimble in the first place!" The goblins began protesting loudly, but Zadie held up her wand for silence. "We'll start our lessons as soon as I've returned my thimble to Fairyland," she said firmly. "But for now . . ."

Rachel and Kirsty smiled as another

burst of fairy magic from Zadie's wand
created matching green vests for all the
other goblins. The goblins whooped with
joy and they put the vests on. They all
walked off, admiring themselves. Zadie
laughed and flew back to Rachel and
Kirsty.

"It's time for me to go home now," Zadie said happily. "Girls, I can't thank you enough! You've been complete superstars. Everyone in Fairyland is going to be so excited when I tell them that you've helped us again. Good-bye—see you very soon!"

"Good-bye," the girls called. Zadie disappeared in a shower of sparkles, waving her thimble at them in farewell.

"Let's take all these green things back to Artie's workshop," Rachel suggested, pointing at the goblins' booth.

The girls quickly gathered everything and hurried through the market square. When they arrived back at the sewing workshop, they were both relieved to see that everyone, including Artie, was looking a lot happier.

"Girls, our sewing projects are back on track!" Artie called to them. "Oh, what a wonderful pile of materials you've collected."

"Looks like everything's OK now that Zadie has her thimble again," Rachel whispered to Kirsty, picking up her half-finished shoulder bag.

"At least now my poor little teddy bear won't lose his stuffing!" Kirsty joked.

Later that day, the girls rushed back to Daffodil Cottage. They couldn't wait to show Mrs. Tate their sewing projects.

"What a gorgeous shoulder bag, Rachel!" Mrs. Tate exclaimed. "I love the velvet flower on the front. And that's such a sweet teddy bear, Kirsty. Great work, you two."

Rachel and Kirsty beamed proudly at each other.

"I've been working on a sewing project of my own while you were gone," Mrs. Tate went on. She handed each of the girls a beautiful pink art apron with purple ties.

"Oh, Mom, these are awesome!" Kirsty gasped. "Look, Rachel, our names are embroidered on the front."

"I love it!" Rachel declared, trying her apron on immediately. "We can wear them whenever we do arts and crafts, Kirsty."

"I'm so glad you like them," said Mrs. Tate with a smile. "Now, should I try sewing that loose button on your shirt again, Kirsty?"

Kirsty shook her head. "No, thanks, Mom. Now that Rachel and I have learned to sew, we're going to do it ourselves," she said with a grin.

The girls ran upstairs to Kirsty's room, still admiring their aprons. But when Kirsty pulled the shirt out of her closet, she gave a cry of surprise.

"Rachel, look! The button's already been sewn back on—with *really* sparkly thread!"

"Fairy magic!" Rachel laughed. "And see, there's something else—a special, sparkly message from Zadie. It's stitched inside the hem of the shirt."

"It says '*thank you*.'" Kirsty grinned at

her friend. "Isn't that amazing, Rachel? I'm so glad we helped another one of the fairies find her magic object."

"Let's hope we can find the others in time to save Crafts Week from total disaster!" added Rachel.

THE MAGICAL CRAFTS FAIRIES

Rachel and Kirsty have found Kayla's,
Annabelle's, and Zadie's missing magic
objects. Now it's time for them
to help

Josie
the Jewelry Fairy!

Join their next adventure
in this special sneak peek. . . .

Golden Seashells

Rachel Walker sat up and yawned, then smiled as she remembered where she was. It was early in the morning, but the sun was already soaking through the canvas of her tent. She looked over at her best friend, Kirsty Tate, who was still curled up in her sleeping bag. So far, their vacation on Rainspell Island had been full of adventure!

"I wonder what today will bring," she whispered to herself.

Rachel leaned back on her pillow and thought about everything that had happened since they'd arrived. It was Crafts Week on the island, and so far the girls had tried pottery, drawing, and sewing. There were lots more crafts left to try, plus a competition and exhibition at the end of the week.

Things had got even more exciting when they met Kayla the Pottery Fairy, though. Rachel and Kirsty were secret friends with all the fairies. Now they were spending spring break together on their favorite island, and they were in the middle of a magical adventure!

Kirsty stirred in her sleep and rolled over. Rachel sat up and unzipped the tent flap. Sunlight spilled into the tent, turning everything golden. Kirsty yawned and opened her eyes.

"Good morning," she said, stretching her arms. "I was having a great dream. I think I sleep even better in the tent than I do in the bed and breakfast!"

Kirsty's family was staying at a little b and b in the village and Rachel's family was camping. The girls had decided to spend every other night at each place all week, and it was turning out to be a lot of fun!

"I think I can hear Mom making breakfast," said Rachel, wriggling out of her sleeping bag. "Come on, I'm starving!"

The girls got dressed and pulled on their sandals.

"What crafts should we do today, Rachel?" asked Kirsty.

"Well, you know it's my mom's birthday today," Rachel said. "I'd love to make something to give her later at the party."

Mr. Walker had organized a surprise party for his wife, and the girls could hardly wait. Just then, there was a tap on the tent flap.

"Come in!" said Rachel and Kirsty together.

Mr. Walker came into the tent and put a finger to his lips. He looked very excited.

"I just want to show you the present I got for your mom," he whispered to

Rachel. "I had them handmade by Carrie Silver, who runs the jewelry shop down by the waterfront."

He held out a tiny velvet box. Rachel took it and opened the lid. Sitting on a bed of ivory silk was a pair of gold earrings shaped like seashells.

"They're beautiful," she said in a soft voice.

"Really pretty," Kirsty agreed.

Rachel picked up one of the earrings—but then something awful happened. The seashell fell off of the rest of the earring. It was broken!

RAINBOW magic ™

Which Magical Fairies Have You Met?

- ❑ The Rainbow Fairies
- ❑ The Weather Fairies
- ❑ The Jewel Fairies
- ❑ The Pet Fairies
- ❑ The Dance Fairies
- ❑ The Music Fairies
- ❑ The Sports Fairies
- ❑ The Party Fairies
- ❑ The Ocean Fairies
- ❑ The Night Fairies
- ❑ The Magical Animal Fairies
- ❑ The Princess Fairies
- ❑ The Superstar Fairies
- ❑ The Fashion Fairies
- ❑ The Sugar & Spice Fairies
- ❑ The Earth Fairies

📖 SCHOLASTIC

HiT entertainment

Find all of your favorite fairy friends at
scholastic.com/rainbowmagic

RMFAIRY10